Ship Shapes

Written by Stella Blackstone   Illustrated by Siobhan Bell

Barefoot Books
Celebrating Art and Story

All aboard! Come along with me!

Let's see what shapes we can find on the sea.

Square

Circle

Triangle

Star

Rectangle

Semi-circle

Diamond

Crescent

Oval

What are the shapes of these sails?

What can you see on this steamboat?

And on this wild sea monster's tail?

What are the shapes of these small fish?

What shape is this green submarine?

And this treasure that twinkles and gleams?

Now that our voyage is over,
It's time to sail quietly home.

Let's have a look all around us

And count up the shapes we've been shown.

For my mother, with much love — Stella Blackstone
For Maureen Guilfoyle — Siobhan Bell

Barefoot Books
2067 Massachusetts Ave
Cambridge, MA 02140, USA

Barefoot Books
124 Walcot Street
Bath, BA1 5BG, UK

This book has been printed on 100% acid-free paper. Graphic design by Judy Linard, London
Photography by Jonathan Fisher Photography, Bath. Reproduction by Grafiscan, Verona
Printed and bound in China by PrintPlus Ltd

This book was typeset in 24 point Soupbone Extra Bold
The illustrations were prepared using hand-dyed cotton sheets

Library of Congress Cataloging-in-Publication Data

Blackstone, Stella.
Ship shapes / Stella Blackstone ; [illustrations by] Siobhan Bell.
p. cm.
ISBN 1-905236-34-4 (hardcover : alk. paper) [1. Shape—Fiction.
2. Boats and boating—Fiction. 3. Rafts—Fiction. 4. Stories in rhyme.]
I. Bell, Siobhan, ill. II. Title.
PZ8.3.B5333Shi 2006
[E]—dc22
2005019937

Hardback ISBN 1-905236-34-4

British Cataloguing-in-Publication Data:
a catalogue record for this book is available from the British Library

1 3 5 7 9 8 6 4 2

Barefoot Books
Celebrating Art and Story

At Barefoot Books, we celebrate art and story that opens the hearts
and minds of children from all walks of life, inspiring them to read deeper, search
further, and explore their own creative gifts. We focus on themes that encourage independence
of spirit, enthusiasm for learning, and sharing of the world's diversity. Interactive, playful and
beautiful, our products combine the best of the present with the best of the past to
educate our children as the caretakers of tomorrow.

www.barefootbooks.com